P9-DJV-622

WITHOUT WORDS

Poems by Joanne Ryder
Photographs by Barbara Sonneborn

Sierra Club Books for Children
San Francisco

The Sierra Club, founded in 1892 by John Muir, has devoted itself to the study and protection of the earth's scenic and ecological resources—mountains, wetlands, woodlands, wild shores and rivers, deserts and plains. The publishing program of the Sierra Club offers books to the public as a nonprofit educational service in the hope that they may enlarge the public's understanding of the Club's basic concerns. The point of view expressed in each book, however, does not necessarily represent that of the Club. The Sierra Club has some sixty chapters in the United States and in Canada. For information about how you may participate in its programs to preserve wilderness and the quality of life, please address inquiries to Sierra Club, 730 Polk Street, San Francisco, CA 94109.

First Edition

Library of Congress Cataloging-in-Publication Data

Ryder, Joanne.
          Without words/by Joanne Ryder; photographs by Barbara
Sonneborn.—1st ed.
                    p. cm.
          Summary: A poetic exploration of the ways humans and animals communicate and interact with a touch, a look, or an action.
          ISBN 0-87156-580-3
          1. Human-animal relationships — Juvenile poetry. 2. Nonverbal communication — Juvenile poetry. 3. Children's poetry, American.
[1. Human-animal relationships — Poetry. 2. Nonverbal communication — Poetry. 3. American poetry.] I. Sonneborn, Barbara, ill. II. Title.
PS3568.Y399W58 1995
811'.54 — dc20   94-38052

Book and jacket design by Bonnie Smetts Design
Title lettering by David Gatti
Printed in Singapore

10 9 8 7 6 5 4 3 2 1

Photographer's Acknowledgments

This book grew out of an idea that my friend Jeffrey Masson had several years ago, concerning whether or not animals have feelings. I'm deeply grateful to Jeff for starting me on the road that led to *Without Words*.

I can't say thank you in enough ways to Helen Sweetland, editor-in-chief at Sierra Club Books for Children, who has been infinitely patient, understanding, and supportive throughout this project. It's also been an absolute pleasure working with associate production editor Lynne O'Neil. Special thanks also to publisher Jon Beckmann and the rest of the staff at Sierra Club Books. I'm very grateful, as well, to Laura Miller of Colorarts Photographics, who produced excellent color prints of my photographs.

This book would not have been possible without the continuing support and enthusiasm of Marine World Africa USA, a nonprofit wildlife park in Vallejo, California, that is devoted to increasing the public's understanding and appreciation of our world's wildlife through education, research, and entertainment. Because of their belief in this project, I was able to develop ideas and photograph in their unique environment, for which I am tremendously grateful. I'd like to express my special thanks to director of public relations Jim Bonde, staff photographer Darryl Bush, and the many animal trainers throughout the park, including Chris Austria, Lisa Bonde, Kim Broadfoot-Hussey, Andy Goldfarb, Jeff Gross, Liam Hussey, Steve Johnson, Debra Marin-Cooney, Pat Martin-Vegue, Jim Mullen, Steve Nagle, Maureen O'Keefe, Karen Povey, Paul Povey, Shay-Ann Redfield, and Ron Whitfield.

I'm also indebted to the many other organizations and individuals that allowed me into their homes, onto their farms, into their parks and other facilities to see and photograph the special bond of respect and affection that can exist between animals and humans. Though we were not able to include in this book all of the animals and people I photographed, I would like to express my deepest gratitude to one and all: Hank Armstrong, manager of public relations at Monterey Bay Aquarium in Monterey, California; Becca Bishop, senior public relations representative, and Amy Perry, animal care specialist, at Sea World of Florida in Orlando; Pat Derby and Ed Stewart of the Performing Animal Welfare Society (PAWS) in Galt, California; Diana Dickson, Alan Kinman, and Norma Dickson-Kinman; Lois Flynne; Denise Hashimoto, animal care specialist at Lincoln Park Zoo in Chicago, Illinois; Thomas C. Linley, park manager, and J. P. Garner, animal care specialist, at Homosassa Springs State Wildlife Park in Homosassa, Florida; Anastasia McGeown, trainer at the Dolphin Research Center in Grassy Key, Florida; Miami Seaquarium in Key Biscayne, Florida; Stephanie, David, and Prudence Petersen; Lex Salisbury, director of Lowry Park Zoo in Tampa, Florida; Silver Springs Wildlife Park in Silver Springs, Florida; Mary Spight and Michael Duer; and Corinne and Cody Vieville.

And finally, to Joanne Ryder, the distinguished author of *Without Words*, I happily say this has been a perfect collaboration. It is an honor to share these pages with you.

Someone
smiling
reaches
toward
a warm
and waiting
furry face.
Sometimes,
without words,
we can make
a bridge
to reach
another
unlike us.

Sometimes,
without words,
each finds
a way to touch,
to move, to play,
sharing pleasure
with each other,
learning how much
we really are the same.

Building trust
takes time . . .
until
bare fingers
touch
a ring of teeth.
An open mouth
reveals a
tender tongue.
Two
meet
at the
water's
edge,
greeting,
trusting.

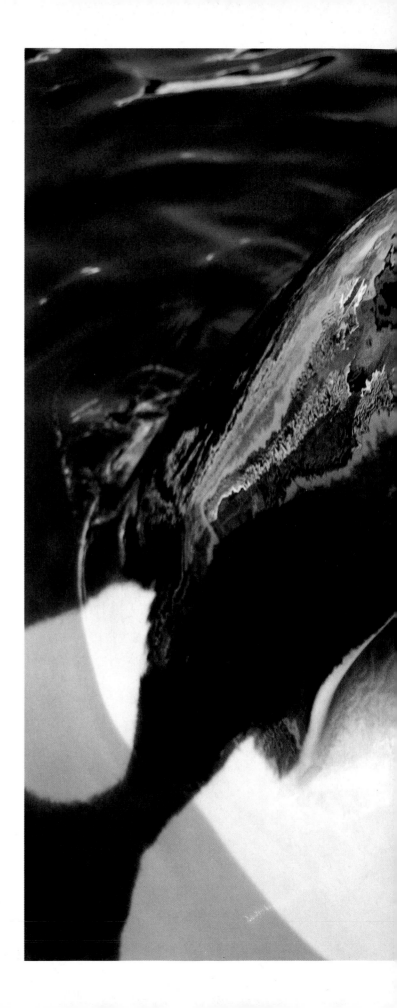

What words
could tell
as much
as a keen
nose sniffing —
or tickle
someone
as gently
as long
wavy whiskers.

A pair
embrace,
arm
and
trunk
entwining,
each
holding
the
other
near
with
tender
firmness.

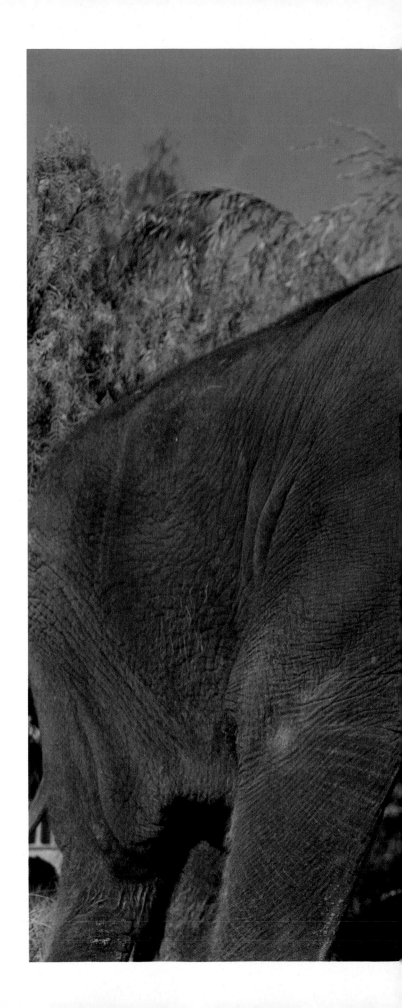

Small arms
wrap
themselves
around
long
caring
arms.
A hug
gives
someone
tired
a place
to rest.

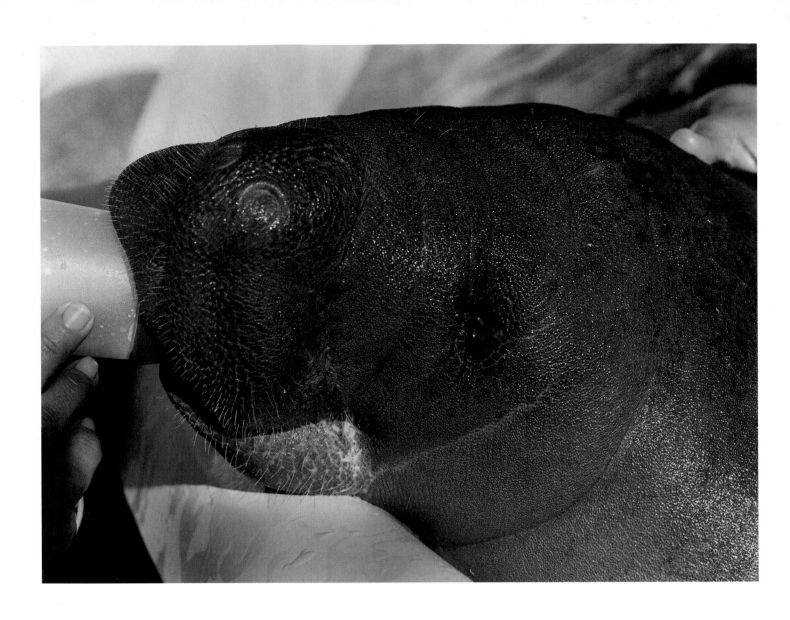

Without a mother's
care and caress,
a young wet one
discovers that hands
can offer milk
and fingers
replace flippers,
rubbing him gently,
showing him
he's not alone.

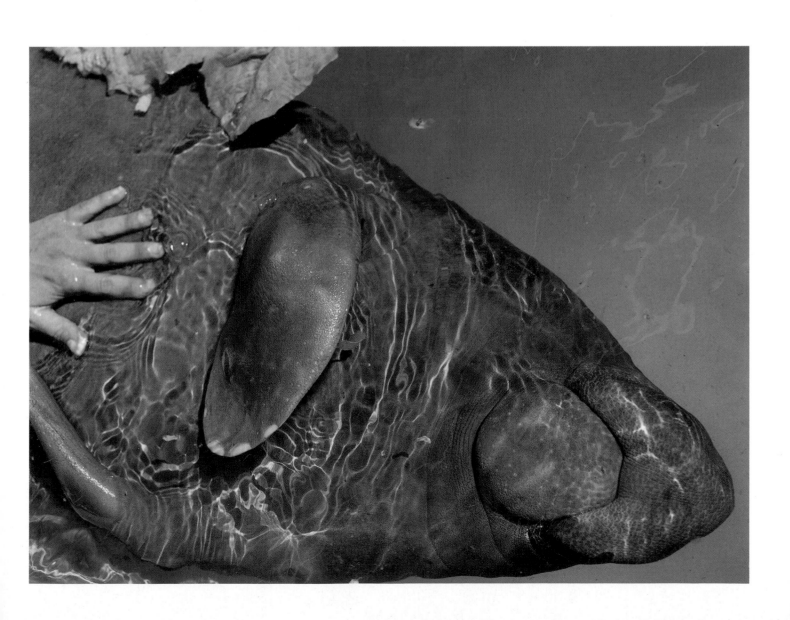

Feeling
the softness
of feathers
against
a cheek,
feeling
the soothing
touch
of hands
under
a wing,
two share
a silent
moment,
calm
and
serene.

Ears high,
young
hunters
watch
and
pounce
and
climb,
enjoying
a game
with
another
who
chooses
to be
down
to
earth
and
playful,
like them.

Sometimes
secrets
can be
shared
with
a look
and
a lick
and
a giggle.

Brilliant
sliders,
bold
gliders
explore
someone
willing,
someone
as brave
and curious
as they.

Without music,
without words,
graceful
partners
dance
their own
special dance
in the
ever-moving
waters.

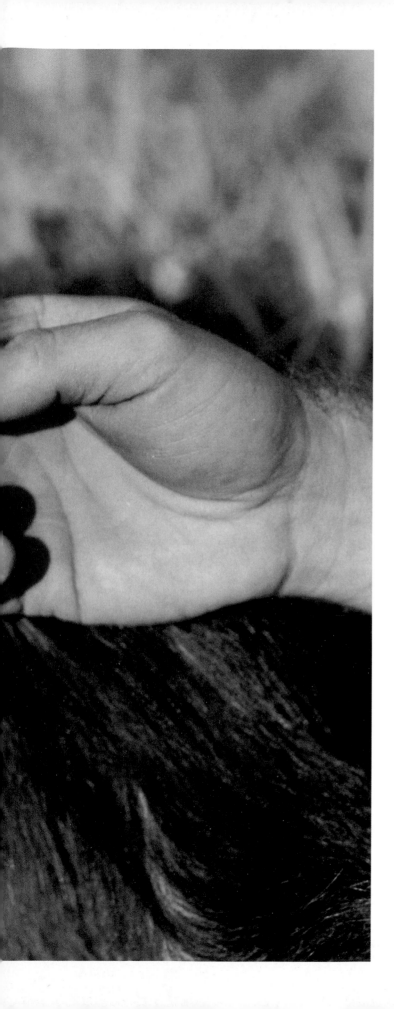

We
touch
each
other
with
small
signs,
small
gestures —
a warm
hand
stroking
a furry
face,
bright
eyes
that
see
and
do
not
turn
away . . .

and
fingers
meshing
in a
bond
no
words
could
make.

Together
we can share
our world,
our lives,
our days,
ourselves —
without
words.

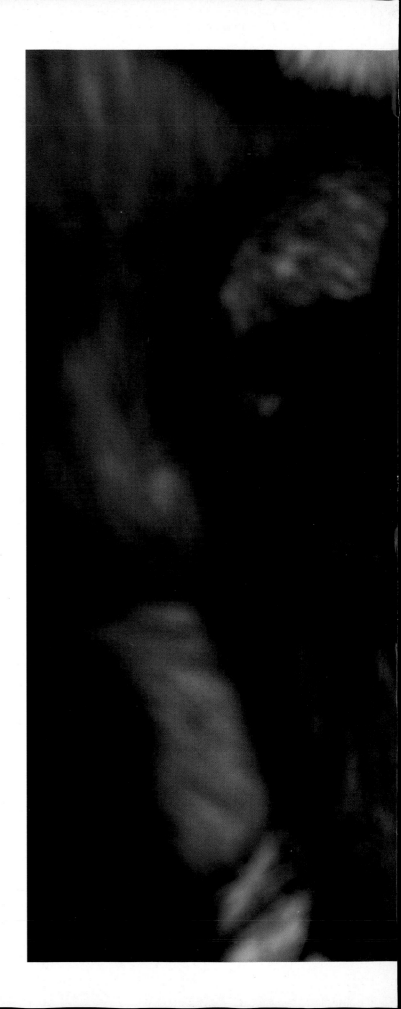

Photographer's Notes

*The information below reflects the status of the animals and their human companions
at the time they were photographed.*

Page 1
Tobey, a young male Bengal tiger, rests on the shoulders of his trainer, Andy Goldfarb. Tobey lives at Marine World Africa USA in Vallejo, California.★

Page 3
Patti, a female chimpanzee, has trainer Liam Hussey check her finger carefully. The five-year-old chimp makes her home at Marine World Africa USA.★

Pages 4-5
Peru, a seven-year-old male llama, lives with his companion, Norma Dickson-Kinman, high in the Colorado Rocky Mountains. A member of the camel family, the llama is native to South America.

Pages 6-7
Five-year-old Kayla, an orangutan, shares a close bond with trainer Steve Nagle at Marine World Africa USA. The orangutan is a primate native only to the islands of Borneo and Sumatra.★

Pages 8-9
Vigga, a female orca, greets trainer Debra Marin-Cooney at the edge of the giant pool at Marine World Africa USA. The eleven-year-old orca weighs in at about 5,000 pounds.

Pages 10-11
Biff, a four-year-old male binturong, spends time with Maureen O'Keefe, a trainer at Marine World Africa USA. The binturong is a tree-dwelling mammal native to Southeast Asia.

Pages 12-13
Judy gives her trainer, Shay-Ann Redfield, an elephant-style hug at Marine World Africa USA. The 8,200-pound Asian elephant is twenty-five years old, and may well live to the age of sixty.★

Pages 14-15
Zawadi, a male African lowland gorilla, rests in the arms of animal care specialist Denise Hashimoto. Now a healthy nine-month-old, Zawadi needed special medical care shortly after he was born at Lincoln Park Zoo in Chicago, Illinois.★

Pages 16-17
Moose is a West Indian manatee—a marine mammal that's distantly related to the elephant. He was an orphan when he was rescued off the west coast of Florida and brought to Sea World of Florida in Orlando. There, animal care specialist Amy Perry gives him lots of love and attention while preparing him for eventual release back into the wild.★

Pages 18-19
Max, a two-year-old African ground hornbill, relaxes in the arms of trainer Lisa Bonde. Max lives in a special environment at Marine World Africa USA.

Pages 20-21
Kahna (left) and Sikari, two female Bengal tiger cubs, play with their trainer, Chris Austria, on Tiger Island at Marine World Africa USA. Though they're just twelve weeks old, the cubs already weigh thirty pounds apiece.★

Pages 22-23
Paws, a male Vietnamese pot-belly pig, frolics with his young companion, Cody Vieville. Paws lives with Cody and his family on their farm in Clayton, California.

Pages 24-25
Two corn snakes—Redoric, a red male, and Cleo, an orange female—twine around Prudence Petersen. Redoric and Cleo live with Prudence and her family in Danville, California.

Pages 26-27
Santini, a female Atlantic bottle-nosed dolphin, swims with trainer Anastasia McGeown in a pool at the Dolphin Research Center in Grassy Key, Florida. Scientists are learning a lot about these curious and intelligent marine mammals through such close interaction.

Pages 28-29
Mikey, a three-year-old chimpanzee, gets an affectionate caress from trainer Liam Hussey. Mikey makes his home at Marine World Africa USA.★

Pages 30-31
Patti (also pictured on page 3) holds hands with trainer Kim Broadfoot-Hussey at Marine World Africa USA.★

★ *Indicates that the species pictured is endangered in the wild*